The Tale of Strawberry Snow

Written by P.L. Caudle
Illustrated by Frank H. Simmonds, IV

Schiffer Publishing Ltd®

4880 Lower Valley Road, Atglen, Pennsylvania 19310

Other Schiffer Books on Related Subjects:

Wild Colt, 978-0-7643-3975-2, $16.99

The True Story of Seafeather, 978-0-7643-3609-6, $14.99

Out of the Sea, Today's Chincoteague Pony, 978-0-87033-595-2, $14.95

Once A Pony Time, 978-0-87033-436-8, $9.95

Designed by Mark David Bowyer
Type set in Aneirin / Teen

ISBN: 978-0-7643-4076-5
Printed in China

Schiffer Books are available at special discounts for bulk purchases for sales promotions or premiums. Special editions, including personalized covers, corporate imprints, and excerpts can be created in large quantities for special needs. For more information contact the publisher:

Published by Schiffer Publishing Ltd.
4880 Lower Valley Road
Atglen, PA 19310
Phone: (610) 593-1777; Fax: (610) 593-2002
E-mail: Info@schifferbooks.com

For the largest selection of fine reference books on this and related subjects, please visit our website at **www.schifferbooks.com**
We are always looking for people to write books on new and related subjects. If you have an idea for a book, please contact us at the above address.

This book may be purchased from the publisher.
Include $5.00 for shipping.
Please try your bookstore first.
You may write for a free catalog.

In Europe, Schiffer books are distributed by
Bushwood Books
6 Marksbury Ave.
Kew Gardens
Surrey TW9 4JF England
Phone: 44 (0) 20 8392 8585; Fax: 44 (0) 20 8392 9876
E-mail: info@bushwoodbooks.co.uk
Website: www.bushwoodbooks.co.uk

To my sister Irene,
the brightest and the best.

On the beautiful island of Chincoteague,
Where cattails and wild willows grow,
There lived a lovely pony.
Her name was Strawberry Snow.

Her coat was as white as
The new fallen snow,
Sprinkled with freckles
Of red all aglow.

She was born in a stall
On a cold winter day,
In a big red barn
By the Chesapeake Bay.

She wobbled about,
And opened her eyes,
Gazed at her mother
In awe and surprise.

The wise old owl,
The barn swallows, too,
The tiny gray mice
Came peeking through.

They came from all over,
Hither and fro',
To get a first glimpse
Of Strawberry Snow.

As they gathered about
Her little straw bed,
Her freckles all glowed
A bright cherry red.

Her shiny red freckles
Lit up the wall,
And cheers of joy
Rang through the stall.

Her tiny hoofs clapped
On the barn's dusty floor,
As she pushed and shoved
At the big wooden door.

She wiggled and tugged till
She poked her nose through.
And for the first time
She saw a bright sky of blue.

Then the door opened wide

And she tumbled outside.

And into the snow,

She started to slide.

It was cold and wet

And the brightest white,

And when she first touched it,

It gave her a fright.

She wanted to run
Out into the snow,
But how her legs trembled
When mother let go!

She kicked up her feet
And pranced all about,
Out the barn door
And past the rain spout.

She hobbled and wobbled
'Til at last she stood
Next to the bin
Where they stored the wood.

She lifted her head
To peek in the bin,
When a friendly spider said,
"Come on in!"

There in the corner,
Still glistening with dew,
Was the loveliest web
All shiny and new.

"Be careful. Don't break it,"
The spider said,
As Strawberry Snow
Slowly lowered her head.

"Spiders are tiny
and freeze when it's cold.
But I'm a brave spider,
I'm very bold."

"I'm big as a snow flake,"
The spider said.
"Too many snow flakes
Would cover my head."

"But I'm a good builder,
As you can see.
I stay in my web
Where I'm safe as can be."

"My name's Oliver
Mortimer Miles," said he.
"Now won't you tell me
What your name might be?"

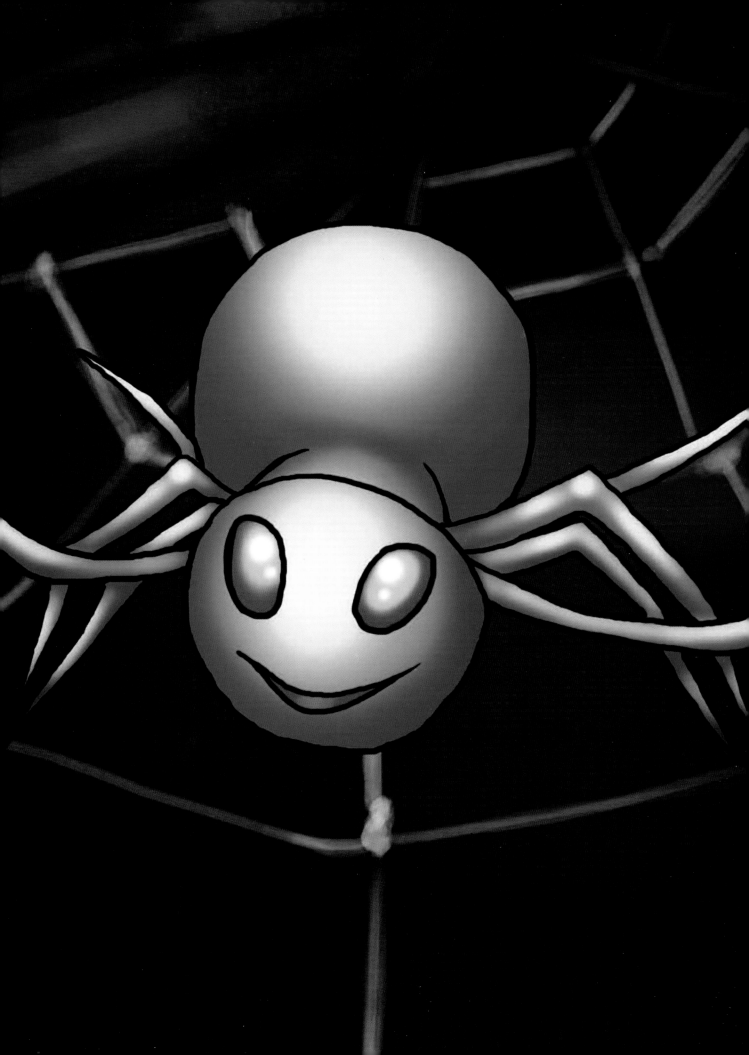

"I'm Strawberry Snow,"
She said very shy.
"I've just come outside
To see the blue sky."

She was prancing about
When she heard mother say,
"Come in. You've had
Enough fun for one day."

But Strawberry Snow
Didn't want to come in.
She wanted to stay
Near Oliver's bin.

Then her tears fell like rain,

As tear drops do.

And lo and behold...

...Her freckles turned blue!

"Now don't you cry,"
Oliver smiled in the bin.
"Come tomorrow morning,
You'll be back again!"

"You must go home now,
You cannot stay.
Tomorrow I'll come out and play."

And the very next morning
When she peeked in...

...She found her new friend
On his web in the bin.

And to this very day,
Strawberry Snow plays
Near the web in the bin
Where Oliver stays.

The
End